About the Author

Dr. Gerloch retired in 1999 from a career as academic and research scientist in the field of quantum chemistry in the University of Cambridge. He is an Emeritus Fellow of Trinity Hall. He and his wife, Gwyneth, have since lived in Canberra, Australia. During his first twenty years of blissful retired domesticity, Malcolm has enjoyed gardening, house renovation and above all, learning to cook in several cuisines. Gwyneth has relinquished the kitchen with mixed feelings. Prior to writing (mostly) children's books, Malcolm's greatest achievement has been the construction of a dual-manual harpsichord for his wife to play. That was a present to thank her for introducing him to the non-scientific literature of – mostly – the nineteenth and twentieth century European and twentieth century North American writers.

About the Illustrator

Angela Hillier studied design publicity and display, watercolours and calligraphy. She worked as a visual aids artist for the Central Electricity Generating Board. After emigrating from the UK to Australia, she spent twenty years in early childhood education, mainly in the Montessori system. Angela is a life member of the Canberra Calligraphy Society and is scribe to the ACT Chief Minister, Governors-General, Parliament House and various Prime Ministers. She has taught calligraphy for many years in the ACT.

BIRD

Malcolm Gerloch

BIRD

Nightingale Books

A CIP catalogue record for this title is
available from the British Library.
ISBN 9781912021 47-5

Nightingale Books is an imprint of
Pegasus Elliot MacKenzie Publishers Ltd.
www.pegasuspublishers.com

First Published in 2019

Nightingale Books
Sheraton House Castle Park
Cambridge England

Printed & Bound in Great Britain

In memory of Morris and Milo

Acknowledgements

Malcolm wishes to thank Liz Hilhorst for her acute criticism and warm encouragement in the early stages of writing this story; also, Gemma Dean-Furlong for her subsequent professional editorial advice, some of which was taken!

Above all, he thanks his wife, Gwyneth, for her endless patience, encouragement, proof-reading and suggestions – many of which were actually taken while others remain to be processed!

Tigger Jumps the Fence

Those pesky dogs! Tigger had enjoyed a calm, dignified and quiet life until those two Corgis appeared. It's not that they were bullies. Far from it, for they couldn't have been more friendly. They were always bouncing up to him, licking him, nuzzling him and urging him to join in their play. But a cat of some years needs peace and quiet. Time to stretch. Time to think about the world as he snoozes, curled up in a ball. Everyone knows that surely, thought Tigger, as he unrolled, stretched and then rolled up the other way. He had climbed over the fence into the garden next door and was sunning himself on hot paving stones on the other side, out of sight and out of reach of those two young puppies. They couldn't see him through the fence, had lost interest and gone to play elsewhere. 'Ah! Peace at last,' thought Tigger.

The same thing had happened three days in a row and Bird had observed it all. Bird was a currawong who ruled over those two gardens and nothing happened that he didn't know about. 'I know everything,' Bird told anyone who would listen, and even some who wouldn't. You might have heard him call out early in the morning? Always loud enough to wake you up.

'I know everything, I know everything.' Mind you, just because he *said* he knew everything didn't mean he really did. But he did have a very loud voice and was proud of his authority.

Tigger was nearly asleep when Bird hopped down onto the stones beside him. Bird liked projects and, right now, he had a new one.

'You should jump that fence for good, Cat,' said Bird. 'You'll have those dogs all over you every day if you don't. The little girl on this side likes you and will feed you.'

'How do you know?' asked Tigger. It was usually quite difficult to catch Tigger's attention but the mention of food worked wonders. And he liked being stroked, of course.

'I know everything,' replied Bird with all his proud authority. Tigger turned over and curled up to think about it. No need to hurry these decisions.

But the next day, after the dogs urged him to play with them, he jumped over the fence again and went on a deliberate, slow, and slinky exploration of the new garden and house. He came across some steps on the other side of the building which led to a small deck outside a glazed door. He was having a good sniff around to check for other cats and found no sign when a little girl appeared on the other side of the door. She quietly slid open the door and spoke to Tigger in such gentle tones that he decided to hang around for a while. After a while, she bent down and stroked him gently on his head and back. 'Ooo! That's good,' he thought and allowed her to do it again.

'Wait there,' she said, 'and I'll get something for you.' After a minute, she returned with a saucer of milk which she put down on the deck in front of the cat.

'Better and better,' thought Tigger and began lapping up the lovely cool liquid. More strokes. 'If this continues, I might wake up completely,' he mused.

'I'm Emma,' the little girl told him and tried to pick him up.

'That's too much for a first date,' thought Tigger, who wriggled free and began to stroll off.

'Do come back sometime,' Emma called after him.

A little while later, when Tigger was curled up on those warm paving stones once more, Bird joined him again. 'Told you!' barked Bird, triumphantly. 'I said she would be nice. I saw it all. I know everything.' Bird was wise enough to know that he mustn't push his new project too hard.

'I'm still thinking about it,' Tigger replied quietly. 'No need to rush these things.'

But next day, he went round to those steps again and found a saucer of fishy food and he tucked into it with relish. He took his time though, for it's undignified for cats to rush their food. 'Not like dogs,' he thought, disdainfully. Just as he was finishing this tasty dish, Emma appeared and opened the door. She had been watching for the cat's arrival for some time.

'Hello again!' she exclaimed. 'I'm so pleased that you came back. I wonder if you'd like to live here permanently. I shall ask Mrs Peters over the fence if that would be OK.' She stroked Tigger for a while and he began to purr his pleasure and agreement with her proposal.

Back on those warm stones, Tigger was sunning himself as Bird flew in to reassure the cat that all would be well in his new life. 'Told you! I know everything,' he told the cat. Tigger purred. He thought that Bird was very wise.

Good Digs

Some while after moving into his new home – for Mrs Peters had agreed – Tigger had found a new spot in the garden on which to sun himself. It was a bare patch of ground not far from those steps up to the deck outside the glazed door and the kitchen. He would curl up one way or the other on it, or stretch out on his back to scratch himself with the soil. From there, he could keep an eye on that door and the chance of more food. He was fed early in the morning and in the late afternoon but you never knew when some extra treat might appear. Tigger wasn't keen on actually doing things but he could keep half an eye open for treats while snoozing and thinking of great things.

Bird would join him while he was having these big thoughts (Tigger couldn't remember what the thoughts were though) and one day told him about the garden and how important he was. They were becoming firm friends by now.

'This is a lovely garden, Cat. We currawongs are so lucky to live here. You too. There are lots of trees, big ones and small. And some are fruit trees. I particularly like figs when they're in season. I can sit on the very tops of those nicholii gums and watch everything that's going on so that, when the figs ripen, I can make sure that none of my cousins get them. My brothers and sisters help to see to that. This is *our* garden these days and I'm the boss. We can hop from those high branches onto the power cables. We call the cables our "social club" because they are a good place to meet our cousins. We allow some into the garden but not others.'

'Who?' asked Tigger.

'We don't mind the silly little peewees,' Bird explained.

'Why are they silly?' asked Cat.

'Have you heard them?' answered Bird.

'Nuff said.' Tigger replied, remembering their weak cries

'A few years ago, the place was taken over by cockatoos, you know,' Bird continued. 'Not all the time, you understand, but just for short visits when they arrived in large numbers. I remember how they inspected the

15

blood-plum tree every day for weeks to tell how well the fruit were ripening. So were the humans.'

Cat looked puzzled.

'No, Cat, I don't mean ripening; I mean watching!'

'Which humans were those?' asked Cat, who was getting quite interested in Bird's story.

'Emma's mother and father,' replied Bird. 'They seem nice enough, by the way.

'One afternoon, those humans came out into the garden with some large baskets and picked every plum from the tree. Every last one was plucked. The tree was stripped! Early next morning, the cockatoos came to inspect the plums, as usual. Their leader settled into the upper branches. After only a moment, he let out a tremendously loud squawk, the like of which I have never heard before or since! He yelled; he swore. He just couldn't believe it. He had looked after those plums for weeks and he and his mates were ready to fill their stomachs and strip the whole tree. For he knew that today was the day. And now, there were none left! He knew who had done the foul deed, he knew who had beaten them to the punch. They were the cockatoos' plums, surely. They had the right! But there was nothing they could do about it. The humans laughed at his squawking and yelling, which only made him madder still. He wouldn't forget. Cockatoos don't forget. You know that, Cat.'

'I just allow the humans to feed me my favourite things,' said Cat in a somewhat superior tone. 'It works for me.'

'All right for some,' grumbled Bird. But he remembered Cat's remark.

'Anyway,' Bird continued. 'Later, the humans put seed into a group of bird-feeders which were like baskets, hanging one above the other, on a chain from one of the nicholii. They watched the cockatoos come in huge numbers. You could see them climbing down the chain, six or more at a time. Cockatoos are messy eaters and they sprayed half the seed all over the ground and the following spring, green shoots appeared all over the place! Much to my surprise, Cat, the humans seemed not to mind these awful table manners. But when one of the cockatoos snipped off the tops of their favourite plants, those humans quite lost their tempers. They shouted at the cockatoos who couldn't understand what was wrong. After all, that was the sort of thing that cockatoos do. They have been called flying secateurs, after all. You know what secateurs are, don't you, Cat? They are like scissors for cutting twigs in the garden.'

'Well, the very next day, Emma's father appeared with a plastic water cannon and began to shoot water at the cockies who were happily resting in the branches of the nicholii. The cockatoos just laughed and squawked at him and flew up to the higher branches where his water spray couldn't reach. But her dad walked up to the tree and fired his cannon straight up and, much to the cockies' surprise and discomfort, he got two of them full in the face! They were most annoyed and squawked at him again and again, flying off to another tree. Emma's dad followed them and kept shooting. It was like a battlefield. Cockatoos do not like getting wet like that and they felt ashamed. They flew off and out of the garden. However, they returned the next day to show their bravery. But the same thing happened. Her father followed them around the garden with shouts and cannon for quite a long time. Again, they flew off. And, again, they returned the following day. Cockatoos have some pride, after all. But it all started up once more and they had to fly off for a third time. They did not return after that.'

'So, the humans won?' asked Cat.

'Yes,' Bird replied, 'but every year, a single cockatoo flies in and inspects the hanging baskets for a moment, finds nothing worthwhile, and flies off for another year. As far as we currawongs are concerned, that's fine for we now have the garden to ourselves. But it shows you how long cockatoos' memories are. We like it here. It's a great home. This is *our* garden now and I'm in charge, Cat.'

Tigger had some vague memories of seeing rozellas, pigeons, galahs, magpies and even kookaburras in the garden but he was too polite to say so to his friend.

Flying

'Look! That currawong is attacking Tigger!'

It certainly seemed so. Tigger was sitting upright on his favourite patch of bare ground in the back garden in full view from the kitchen window. A currawong was circling around him, gently swooping towards and away from him while the cat pawed the air with a sort of paddling motion. The cat suddenly jumped up into the air. The currawong put on its air-brakes and landed right in front of him.

'Why doesn't Tigger grab him now while he can?' Emma's father was saying. The bird hopped up and down around the cat which turned this way and that to watch its every move. The bird was gently flapping its wings as it hopped. Tigger pawed the air again but made no attempt to catch the bird. When the currawong came round in front of the cat again, it hopped into the air and flew almost vertically for about a metre and then dropped gently back down to the ground. The cat pawed the air again. The bird flew up a short way once more before gliding back to the ground in front of the cat.

This all took quite a time. 'Tigger doesn't seem to mind. I think the currawong is dancing for him!' Emma said, but neither she nor her father could hear what the bird was saying. And they didn't realise, of course, that Bird had a new project.

'Come on Cat,' Bird was saying. 'You can do it. Just keep trying. Flap your wings, hop up off the ground, push out your chest and FLY! It's a wonderful feeling. Watch me again. I'll show you how to zoom up to that branch on the gum tree. It's so easy once you get the confidence. You can bank to the right or the left and then gently glide all the way down. Come on, Cat; try it.'

'I'm trying, I'm trying, but nothing seems to happen. I don't think I have the gift. What makes you think I can learn to fly?'

'Trust me, Cat; I know everything,' said the bird. 'We both have yellow eyes for a start and that must be important.'

'Let me tell you again about the wonder of flight. I arch my back, push out my chest and with a few big flaps of my wings, I soar away. It feels like wallowing in a bath of air. I swoop, I float, I dive. How lovely to feel the air rushing past. And what views I get of the tree-tops, of the whole garden – and even of the gardens next door. Sometimes, I fly further afield and have a sticky-beak at what's going on in gardens and bush much further away.'

'You're getting quite poetical, Bird,' said the cat, still wagging his front elbows around. But he wasn't having much success with his flying.

'I always know what you are doing, Cat, because I can see you from a long way away. I can fly fast; I can fly slowly. I come to you in one long glide and I then use my air-brakes to land right next to you. Mind you; some of my cousins can fly much faster than me. They are just show-offs, though. They make a bee-line for some tree branch at the other end of the garden and fly so fast, almost in a straight line, banking to the right to avoid that twig, to the left to go round that flower. They love flying fast. They seem to have a need, a need for speed. Sometimes, they "buzz" a human as they scoot past his ear on their high-speed dash. They're hooligans, really. Oh, Cat! You must learn to fly. You would enjoy it so much.'

'You nearly flew into that curly tree branch just then, Bird,' said Cat.

'No, I didn't. No, I didn't. I saw it in good time. I had planned to change direction like that. Don't you worry, Cat. I know everything.'

Losing Cat

Another year passed.

Cat was eating his breakfast which Emma had put out on a saucer for him. A currawong – yes, it *was* the same one but Emma could not be sure – had perched on a fence rail just behind the eating cat. The cat ignored the bird but knew it was there. Cat was very ill; actually, he was dying. Cat knew it and Bird knew it. Emma and her parents probably knew it but you can never be sure with humans. Cat ate slowly while Bird patiently waited up on the fence rail. Cat finished and moved forward a short way on the deck, leaving a little food on his saucer. Bird hopped down onto the deck right next to Cat and tucked into the leavings. Cat totally ignored what was going on as if he didn't know, but he did, of course. The humans looked on with some amazement but began to understand after a while. Humans can be slow sometimes.

'Tigger and the currawong seem to be friends,' they said. Obviously. Breakfast happened the same way every day.

One morning, a beautiful, foreign cat crept slowly up towards the deck where Cat was eating his breakfast but went away after a short while. It was just having a quick look. But the next day, the foreigner came back and climbed the seven steps onto the deck where Cat was finishing his meal. It pushed his way towards the saucer and it knew that Cat was ill, if not dying. Cats know these things by instinct, and it pushed Cat aside to rob him of his food. Cat yelled loudly in protest but was too weak to defend himself. Bird squawked as loudly as he could, again and again. He began pecking at the foreigner's back until it ran off at full speed towards the fence at the end of the garden. As it climbed hurriedly over the fence, Bird swooped low, loudly squawking again and pecking at its back. Emma and her mother had heard Bird's squawking and Tigger's cries. By the time they reached the glazed door to the deck, they just managed to see Bird chasing off the intruder. They applauded Bird enthusiastically.

Tigger was very upset by the attack. In days gone by, he would have seen off the intruder immediately; no worries. But Cat was ill now, dying, and couldn't manage to defend himself any more. Bird understood completely.

The next day, Bird saw the foreigner coming back by way of the garden next door and swooped low over it, squawking and pecking at him with his strong beak. No matter how fast that cat ran, he couldn't shake off Bird, who kept on attacking. The foreigner didn't try again.

Cat took to living on the roof of the humans' nest, though. He still had enough strength – and courage – to jump about a metre from a front wall onto a low part of the roof. From there, he would wander all over the roof of the humans' nest, night and day alike, only coming down (actually being carried down by the humans) at meal-times. He felt safe on the roof but it wasn't right that he should be frightened off from his rightful patch.

Bird often visited Cat on the roof though, so that was all right. Bird reminded Cat of how he had persuaded him to jump the fence and escape the over-enthusiastic dogs next door. 'I was right about your being happy over here,' he said proudly.

Cat agreed with Bird and told his friend so. On one occasion, Bird took a worm for Cat to eat up on his roof. Cat wasn't keen on that, though.

One evening, sometime later, several humans gathered at the back door near the deck where Cat would breakfast. One of them was carrying Cat in their arms. They all seemed very upset. Cat was taken away. Bird didn't see him again.

'But I do know that Cat is flying now in his heaven. I taught him, you know,' Bird was telling his missus. Then,

'Do you think the humans will get another cat?' he asked her.

'Of course they will,' she replied.

'When? How do you know?' asked Bird.

'Soon. Trust me. I know everything,' replied his missus.

Now that was something that Bird really understood.

Feeding Time

It had been more than a year since Cat had left this world. Bird asked his missus for the hundredth time whether she still expected to see a new cat in the humans' nest. The place didn't seem right without one. 'Oh, yes, I'm sure they'll get one very soon,' she said. 'We'll just have to be patient.'

Bird had a new project. He had remembered Cat saying a long time ago that he graciously allowed the humans to feed him. Bird decided to find out if Cat's human friends remembered his part in helping Tigger against the foreign cat. Early one morning – but not too early, because humans seem far lazier than birds – he flew onto the fence rail next to the deck where Cat used to eat and share his breakfast. It took but one short hop to land on a narrow ledge right outside the kitchen window. Bird knocked on the window with his long, strong beak.

Tap, tap. No, come on, louder than that. Currawongs aren't shy, for goodness' sake. More a *knock, knock*.

After a while, Emma came to find out what or who was making the noise. *Knock, knock*, repeated Bird. The little girl – who was not so little now, by the way – spoke to Bird: things like, 'Hello,' and 'How are you?'

Knock, knock, went Bird again, thinking, 'How about some food? It's nesting time.' He really did need the extra food at this time of year.

'Aren't you the bird who helped Tigger last year? I do believe you are,' said Emma. 'Wait a minute.'

'Aha,' thought Bird. 'I think it's going to work.' *Knock, knock.*

'Yes, yes, wait a minute,' said Emma and busily tore up a piece of bread into a saucer. She moistened the bread with a little water – for she knew how hot the sun would get in a while. She opened the door and put the saucer down on the deck.

'Come on, help yourself.'

Bird had already hopped off the window ledge back onto the fence rail as soon as he saw the door about to open. One more hop and he was on the deck and, as soon as the door closed, he went right up to the saucer and took a piece of bread. It was a seeded bread. 'Oh, good.' After eating two more pieces, Bird took a large piece in his beak but, holding it there without swallowing, flew up onto the fence rail and from there up and away into the trees to the left. When he was sure nobody was watching – and he knew how sharp his brothers' and cousins' eyes could be – he flew off in a completely different direction to the place where his missus was beginning to build a new nest. He gave the large piece of bread to her. Straight away, he flew back to the saucer, but by a roundabout route, to take more bread for himself and for his missus. And so it went, until all the bread was gone.

Bird waited till late afternoon before trying again. *Knock, knock. Knock, knock.*

'All right, all right,' cried Emma. 'I'm coming. I'm at your *beak* and call!'

This time though, she added a few green grapes to the saucer of bread pieces.

'Things are looking up,' thought Bird but he had a little difficulty swallowing the rather large grapes. He did manage, but Emma saw how difficult it was. Even so, Bird flew off with a grape in its beak to give to his missus.

Something very similar happened the next morning and, indeed, every morning for several weeks. But when grapes appeared, Bird found that they had been cut in two so he had no difficulty swallowing them anymore. He told his missus that the girl had cut the grapes in two with a knife.

'How do you know that?' she asked him.

'I know everything,' he replied. He had watched the human cutting up the grapes through the window. What did you think?

A few days later, Bird brought his missus along with him to perch on the fence by the breakfast deck. The girl put out the saucer with bread and grapes. Bird took half a grape from the saucer and flew up to the fence rail and his missus. He popped the half grape into her open beak as if he were feeding a baby. Emma and her mother were standing behind the glazed door to the deck, happily watching the whole thing. 'I knew they would,' thought Bird with a grin. Birds can grin but it's difficult for humans to see them doing it. So that's all right.

They flew off together when they had finished the saucer. Only they knew where their nest was. Although his missus was the one to build it, they chose the place together. In the past, when they mostly lived in the bush nearby, they would select a place between branches high above ground. But now that they lived around houses and had grown used to humans – particularly to Cat's humans – they had chosen a place in a fairly thick, flowering bush which was growing under a high deck on the other side of the humans' nest. It was pretty dry under there and very well hidden from both the house windows and from the open spaces outside. Bird was really proud of their choice of where to live. Of course, being so close to the humans' nest meant that they knew immediately when there was a chance of another feed. As Bird kept saying to his missus, 'I know everything.'

Here Come the Newbies

In due course, Bird and his missus were so happy to become parents again. Two eggs had hatched and they were very proud of a new son, who they called Coo, and a new daughter, Ee. But now there were four mouths to feed and Bird had to work hard while the missus watched over the young 'uns in the nest. And when those little 'uns were hungry – which was very often – they would yell at the tops of their little voices. Bird came to depend a lot on the extra food given by the humans and he would race back and forth – actually from the back of the house to the front, as we know – with softened bread to put into the yelling mouths of their babies. The humans seemed well aware of what was going on, if not exactly where, and were more than happy to provide breakfasts and suppers every day.

Meanwhile, and just as Bird's missus had promised, the house got a cat presence once more. But there were *two* cats! They were kittens called Flea, a girl with soft, black and white fur and a very sweet face with hazel, green eyes; and a boy, Ridden, with yellow eyes and magnificent, marmalade-coloured fur like Tigger's. They were always scratching themselves and when they were naughty, which was very often indeed, the humans would call out to them, 'Flea, Ridden: do behave.' Not that that made any difference, of course. With his very sharp, yellow eyes,

Bird could see the humans playing with the kittens inside the house.

He reported back to his missus, 'Ridden and Flea dash after a soft toy which the humans toss onto the rug in front of them but they always run so quickly that, when they put their brakes on at the last minute, they tumble head over heels. That makes the humans squeal with delight. Then they run up and down the curtains.'

'What?' asked his missus.

'No! The kittens, not the humans,' he laughed at her. 'Anyway, that didn't amuse the humans half as much. "Flea, Ridden; behave," they yell. Those kittens are very naughty.'

'I think the time has come for our two newbies to learn to fly,' Bird's missus said one day. So now Bird had another new project.

'Coo, Ee,' they called. 'Time to fly.' The kids were terrified but before they had time to protest, Bird had thrown them out of the nest. It was only a couple of metres from the ground but both Coo and Ee hit the ground with a thud. They squawked in protest but Bird was having none of it.

'You haven't been hurt, you landed on a pile of leaves. Stop your squawking. Now come with me, walk along behind me.' All three walked off to a nearby fence. They were being secretly watched by the humans behind a window. They didn't see the humans – or rather Coo and Ee didn't. Bird did, but was happy to put on a show.

Using his large beak, Bird took hold of Coo by his neck and carried him up to the top of the rush fence. Then he flew down and carried Ee up onto the fence in the same way. Bird then told Coo and Ee how easy it was to fly.

'You arch your back and stick out your chest. You flap your wings and… off you go!' he said and gave each of the kids a smart tap on its back to topple it off the fence. 'Flap your wings!' he yelled at them as they tumbled to the ground. 'You can't fly if you don't flap your wings. You will really love flying. You can soar, you can glide, you can bank… to the left, to the right. It's a wonderful feeling! You can do it. We'll try again.'

And with that, Bird carried Coo and Ee up onto the fence again. Once more, he gently pushed them off. 'Flap your wings. You'll never fly if you don't flap your wings. Come on, get up. We'll try once more.' And again, he carried them up onto the fence. Once more, he told them how to do it but he was getting a little bit irritated. This time, Bird didn't push Coo and Ee off the fence. Instead, he very gently flew off the fence himself, flapping his wings much more quickly than he needed to, to show them what to do. He landed a few metres away and called up to them.

'Now, in your own time, flap your wings and slowly push yourselves up with your legs.' Nothing happened. Coo and Ee just stood on top of the fence and looked at the ground beneath them. 'Come on. You can do it!' cried Bird. Nothing happened. Bird was getting fed up, he was losing his patience. Suddenly, he had an idea. He flew up higher than the top of the fence and swooped down on his kids, flapping his large wings wildly in their faces. They were so startled by this quite unexpected 'attack' that each rocked on its perch, flapped its wings madly, and jumped off the fence. But they kept flapping for a while and so found themselves back on the ground but this time quite a long way from the fence.

'That's it!' yelled Bird. 'You flew, you flew! Now let's do it again but this time, keep flapping your wings and fly up to a tree branch. And we'll start from the ground, from right where you are.'

And so, it came to pass that Coo and Ee learned to fly that day. It took several more goes before they were able to fly up to a tree branch quite far above them. But they did it, and afterwards, they flew behind their father – by a secret route, of course – back to the nest where they fell fast asleep for a long time. Bird was well pleased with them both. And, of course, with himself.

Growing Up

Next morning, around Cat's old breakfast time, Bird announced that it was time to show off Coo and Ee to the humans and for the kids to learn to feed themselves. And so it was, after *knock, knock* and the saucer appearing on the deck, that Bird flew off high into the nicholii and immediately returned with his missus and their kids. The humans were watching from behind the glass door. At first, all four birds perched on the fence rail.

'You can tell how young the kids are,' Emma's father was saying, 'by their fluffy greyish feathers. They're so fluffy that they make the fledglings seem bigger than their parents.'

Bird encouraged Coo and Ee to join him next to the saucer on the deck. Bird leaned forwards and took a piece of bread in his beak and then swallowed it. 'Come on,' he urged the kids. 'You do the same thing.'

Ah, no! Coo and Ee just stood there, quietly screeching, their heads thrown back and their beaks wide open, waiting for Dad to pop some softened bread into them.

'Not this time,' Bird said. 'Now is the time for you to feed yourselves. Copy what I do,' and with that, he bent forward once again and slowly took a piece of bread into his beak, leaned his head back and swallowed. 'Now, you do it,' he urged. Nothing happened. Mum flew down to the saucer and she did what Dad had done so that now the kids had seen both of them do it.

It seemed an age before Ee suddenly leaned forward and picked up a piece of bread. 'Yes, yes; that's it,' cried Bird. Ee dropped the bread on the deck.

Bird showed them the whole thing all over again. This time Coo lifted some bread and… yes! He leaned his head back and opened his beak a little and the bread fell into the pot! 'Good, good!' Dad was so pleased. 'Now you, Ee; you can do it.' And she did. They both did it again. And again. Sometimes, they dropped the bread on the deck but Bird showed them how to clean up. The kids had learned to feed themselves… from a saucer of food from the humans anyway. Emma and her parents had been watching the whole thing and now clapped. Unfortunately, this scared the young birds away, but they came back after a while.

There had been a lot of learning in the last two days but it had all gone very well indeed. After a while, the humans stopped putting anything out for the birds. Coo and Ee had learned to look after themselves now; to eat berries and creepy crawlies from the garden and, especially, fruit. The figs were beginning to ripen and Bird, his family and many of Bird's brothers and sisters were gorging themselves on those lovely fruits.

They were thoughtful, though. They always left a few for the humans on the lower branches where they could reach them!

I Remember

'Those fluffy young 'uns seem to be bothering the kittens,' Emma's mother was saying sometime later.

On that bare patch of ground, some twenty metres from the kitchen window, there was a strange group of two kittens and two young birds. Flea and Ridden were rolling around on the ground in tight circles, sometimes even doing their somersaults while the fluffy grey currawongs were jumping up and down off the ground, and when they landed, rolling around sideways near the kittens. From time to time, the kittens would go up to Coo or Ee and give them a push with their noses to help the birds roll over. There was a lot of wing flapping going on and screeches. Suddenly everything would go quiet and the kittens would seem to nuzzle the currawongs.

'Come on Ee; come on Coo,' Ridden was saying. 'You can do it; it's so easy. It's so much fun! You just curl up into little balls and roll. I'll show you again. Curl up into a little ball. And listen to me now: you can show how happy you are by purring like us. Come close and you can hear how happy we are.' Their motors ran: 'Purrrrr…'

Bird was watching what was going on from high in the nicholii.

'I remember, I remember… Cat used to curl up and go to sleep on that bare patch of ground,' he said to himself.

Life renews but friendships last for ever.